PA 4/19

D0111168

pa

First published in Great Britain 2018 by Red Shed,
an imprint of Egmont UK Ltd
The Yellow Building, 1 Nicholas Road, London W11 4AN

www.egmont.co.uk
Copyright © Egmont UK Ltd 2018

Illustrations by iStock.com/Daria Voskoboeve; iStock.com/n_chetkova;
iStock.com/Kapona; iStock.com/ekmelica; iStock.com/Giuseppe Ramos

ISBN 978 1 4052 9433 1

A CIP catalogue record for this title is available from the British Library.

Stay safe online. Egmont is not responsible for content hosted by third parties.

Egmont takes its responsibility to the planet and its inhabitants very seriously.
We aim to use papers from well-managed forests run by responsible suppliers.

The Ultimate
UNICORN
JOKE BOOK

YOO-HOO-nicorn!

I'm Sparkly Jim – the FUNNIEST unicorn in the magical forest (FACT). I want to welcome you to my glittery rainbow realm to hear my favourite jokes and meet all of my magical friends.

Now it's time for the MANE event . . .
So sit back, put up your hooves and get ready to laugh yourself HORSE!

(Any jokes that don't make you laugh were probably written by wizards.)

Which unicorn lives in space?

The moon-icorn.

What did the mirror say to the unicorn?

I see you-nicorn!

Knock, knock!

Who's there?

U

U who?

Unicorn!

Knock, knock!

Who's there?

The interrupting unicorn

The interr-

Neigh!

Who is the
smelliest unicorn?

The poo-nicorn.

Which unicorn sleeps
until midday?

The noon-icorn.

Which unicorn
loves singing?

The tune-icorn.

Which unicorn
helps you eat
cereal?

The spoon-icorn.

What did the
unicorn say to the
love of his life?

Will you marey me?

Which unicorn always gets forgotten?

The who-nicorn?

Which unicorn has
carriages and runs
on steam?

The choo-choo-nicorn.

Which unicorn
has a cold?

The achoo-nicorn.

Which unicorn can see
into the future?

The fortunicorn teller.

Which unicorn
causes a fuss?

The hullaballoo-nicorn.

Which unicorn is
a cat in disguise?

The mew-nicorn.

What do you say
to a really cool
unicorn?

You're a legend!

What do you
call a unicorn
without a horn?

Pointless.

What do you call
a baby unicorn?

The brand new-nicorn.

I met a really scary unicorn
the other day . . .

Night-mare!

Why did the unicorn
cross the road?

To visit her neighbour.

Where do unicorns throw their rubbish?

In the glitter bin.

Why did the unicorn sneeze?

He had hay fever.

How do
unicorns get around
the magical forest?

On uni-cycles.

What happens when you interrupt a unicorn reading the newspaper?

I don't know, but there'll be some crosswords!

Where do sick unicorns go?

The horse-pital.

Why was the unicorn
hanging out with a lion,
a witch and a wardrobe?

Narnia business!

Did you hear about the
unicorn who made a belt
out of watches?

It was a waist of time.

What do unicorns
wear on their feet?

Horseshoe-nicorns.

Why was the unicorn such a good guitar player?

She knew all the uni-chords.

What did the unicorn say when he fell over?

Help – I can't giddy up!

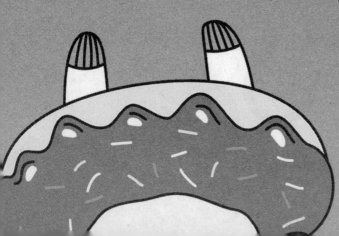

Why couldn't the Shetland
unicorn pay for his shopping?

He was a bit short.

What do unicorns say
when they kiss?

Ouch!

The unicorns are going on
a road trip! Where first?

Canter-bury!

Where did
they go next?

Horsta Rica.

How did they
get there?

They flew-nicorn!

Why do
unicorn cars win
all the races?

*They've got so much
horse-power.*

What happened to
the tiny unicorn?

He grew-nicorn.

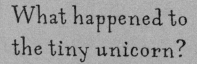

Why are unicorns
not funny?

Their jokes are so uni-corny!

Why was the unicorn arrested?

She was the mane suspect.

How do unicorn drivers overtake?

They use the horn!

What do unicorns say when they see Star Wars?

May the horse be with you!

Did you know that unicorn spit is glittery?

I got it straight from the horse's mouth.

Did you hear about
the unicorn who won the
100m gold medal?

It was a one-horse race.

What do you say
to a unicorn when
they graduate?

Corn-gratulations!

What is a unicorn's favourite
subject at school?

Horse-tory.

What is a unicorn's
favourite thing
about school?

The uni-form.

What is a unicorn's
favourite type
of story?

Fairy tails.

What did the teacher say to the naughty unicorn?

Stop horsing around!

Why did the naughty unicorn get detention?

She used foal language.

Why did the wizard do well at school?

He was so good at spelling.

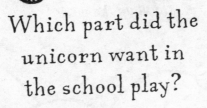

Which part did the
unicorn want in
the school play?

The mane role.

How did the unicorn feel
when the PE teacher told
him to stop heading the ball?

It was deflating.

Why was the
unicorn the star player
of the school football team?

*She was good at hoofing the
ball up the pitch.*

What do unicorns
like to play in PE?

Stable tennis.

Why were
the unicorn team
awarded a penalty?

There was a foal.

What do
unicorns wear at
smart dinner parties?

Rainbow-ties.

What do
unicorns say when
they smell a rainbow?

Hoofarted?

Why was the
team disappointed to
be runners-up?

They wanted to whinny!

Did you hear about the
unicorn who dyed his
hair multicoloured?

It was a mane-bow.

What do unicorn pirates sail in?

A rain-boat.

Which rainbow is like a massive dog?

The Great Dane-bow.

Which rainbow
always goes full
steam ahead?

The train-bow.

Which
rainbow loves
eating tapas?

The Spain-bow.

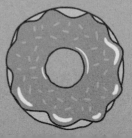

Which
rainbow thinks
a lot of itself?

The vain-bow.

Which rainbow
scores lots of goals?

The Harry Kane-bow.

Which rainbow takes
everyone on holiday?

The aeroplane-bow.

Which rainbow is good at building?

The crane-bow.

Why were the unicorns multicoloured and dripping wet?

It was pouring with rainbow.

What did the unicorn horn say to the scarf?

You stay there, I'll go on a head.

What is a unicorn's
favourite hair style?

A pony tail.

What's a unicorn's
favourite TV show?

Neigh-bours.

What is a unicorn's
favourite dance show?

Strictly Come Prancing.

What is a unicorn's
signature dance move?

The nae nae.

What is a unicorn's favourite football team?

Tottenham Horse-spur.

What is a unicorn's second favourite football team?

Manchester Unicornited.

And who is their
favourite manager?

Horse Mourinho.

Who is a unicorn's favourite member of One Direction?

Niall Horsan.

What is a unicorn's favourite radio station?

Neighdio One.

What is a unicorn's favourite band?

Neighdiohead.

What is
a unicorn's
favourite job
around the house?

Hoovering.

What is a unicorn's
favourite
thing to do?

Watch cartoonicorns.

What is a unicorn's favourite Star Wars film?

The Horse Awakens.

And who is their favourite character?

Princess Neigha.

First unicorn:
What do you think of
the magical forest?

Second unicorn:
It's oakay.

What is the unicorn's
favourite tree in the
magical forest?

The horse chestnut.

How do the unicorns get on the wifi in the magical forest?

They just log on.

First unicorn: I've heard there are talking trees in the magical forest.

Second unicorn: I don't beleaf you!

How do you play magical forest hide-and-seek?

*Close your eyes and
count to tree.*

Why didn't the
unicorn win the game
of magical forest
hide-and-seek?

He was stumped.

What did the trees wear to the magical forest pool party?

Swimming trunks.

Why did the
unicorn fall out
with the tree in the
magical forest?

*The tree was
throwing shade.*

Did you hear
about the unicorn
who ran into a tree in
the magical forest?

Face palm!

What was the magical
forest party like?

Tree-mendous.

What sport do
unicorns play in
the magical forest?

Tree-athlons.

Why were the trees the last ones to leave the magical forest party?

They wooden go.

Did you hear
about the tree that
vanished in the
magical forest?

It was a mys-tree!

First unicorn:
How was the magical
forest sleepover?

Second unicorn:
I slept like a log!

What did
the unicorn say to the
tree in the magical forest?

*Now it's just
yew and me.*

What did
the tree say back
to the unicorn?

*Now it's just
you-nicorn and me.*

What is the difference between a carrot and a unicorn?

One is a bunny feast and the other is a funny beast.

What do you call a small scoop of ice-cream?

A uni-cone.

What do unicorns have for breakfast?

Uni-cornflakes.

A unicorn walked into the Rainbow Sparkle Café.

The owner said, 'Hey, why the long face?'

What is
a unicorn's
favourite food?

*Baked ponytato
with tunicorn mayo.*

What did the unicorn order
in the Italian restaurant?

Spaghetti Bolog-neighs.

What is the most
mythical vegetable?

The uniCORN.

What is good advice at a unicorn picnic?

Don't bite off more that unicorn chew.

What kind of water do unicorns like?

Sparkling.

What do
unicorns eat at
the cinema?

Unipopcorn.

What did the unicorn say when someone tried to take her lunch?

Hay!

What did the corn seller say to the unicorn?

You need corn?

Did you hear about the unicorn who tried to eat a clock?

It was time-consuming.

Two unicorns were
at the magical forest BBQ.

First unicorn: I prefer the
sparkly moon rock burger to
the rainbow burger.

Second unicorn:
Yes, it's a little meteor.

I had dinner with a
time-travelling unicorn
the other night.

*He went back
four seconds.*

Why didn't the
unicorns get in the
pool at the magical
forest BBQ?

*You shouldn't swim on
a foal stomach.*

What else did the
unicorns eat at the
magical forest BBQ?

Unicorn on the cob.

Have you met the unicorn baker?

She's a thorough-bread.

Have you met the vegetarian unicorn?

I've not met herbivore.

What cheese did the unicorn bring to the masked ball?

Mascarpone.

The unicorn knew it was
wrong to steal from the
kitchen. So why did she do it?

*It was a whisk she was
willing to take.*

What did the
greedy little unicorn
say to his friends when she
fancied a midnight feast?

Hoofeels hungry?

What did the greedy little
unicorn say while they were
having the midnight feast?

Hoofinished the cookies?

What did the greedy
little unicorn's dad say
when he found them?

It's past-ure bedtime.

What did the
mermaid say when
the unicorn came
over to her house?

Sea, horse!

Did you hear
about the mermaid
who lies all the time?

*She's always
telling tails.*

What did
the mermaid do
for her birthday?

She had a shellebration.

How did the
mermaid party go?

It went swimmingly.

Did you hear about the grumpy mermaid?

She's very antiso-shell.

Did you hear about the musical mermaid?

She is very good at scales.

When do mermaid spies complete their missions?

When the coast is clear.

Why did the mermaid
call the police?

It was an emergen-sea.

Where do fancy
mermaids live?

In sandcastles.

What is a
mermaid's
favourite
football team?

Chelsea.

What was the
wizard doing in
the magical forest?

*Just wand-ering
around.*

What did the mermaid
bring to the magic picnic?

Sand-wiches.

What did
the wizard bring to
the magic picnic?

Sand-witches

What do
I do when a
mermaid steals
my beach snack?

I scream.

Did you hear
about the witch who
made her whole left
side disappear?

She's all right now.

Did you hear
about the witch who
stole a tractor?

She turned into a field.

Who did
the witch live with?

Her broom-mate.

What did the
unicorn say when the wizard
tried to trick him?

*You won't make a foal
out of me!*

Why did the
cheeky pixie
keep pulling the
unicorn's tail?

He got a kick out of it.

Did you hear
about the pig who
pretended to be a unicorn?

She was telling porkies.

Which unicorn is
a ghost in disguise?

The wooooooooo-nicorn.

Which unicorn is a cow in disguise?

The moo-nicorn.

At the magical forest fancy dress party all the dolphins dressed up as unicorns.

It was fin-tastic.

Did you hear about the T.rex who pretended to be a unicorn?

He stuck out like a saur thumb.

At the magical forest
fancy dress party all the
dogs dressed up
as unicorns.

It was paw-some.

At the magical forest fancy dress party all the frogs dressed up as unicorns.

It was toad-ally awesome.

At the magical forest fancy dress party all the tortoises dressed up as unicorns.

It was a turtle surprise!

Unicorn:
Did you enjoy the jokes?

Wizard:
I thought they were
wand-erful, especially
the ones I wrote!

Unicorn:
Me too – I laughed
myself horse!